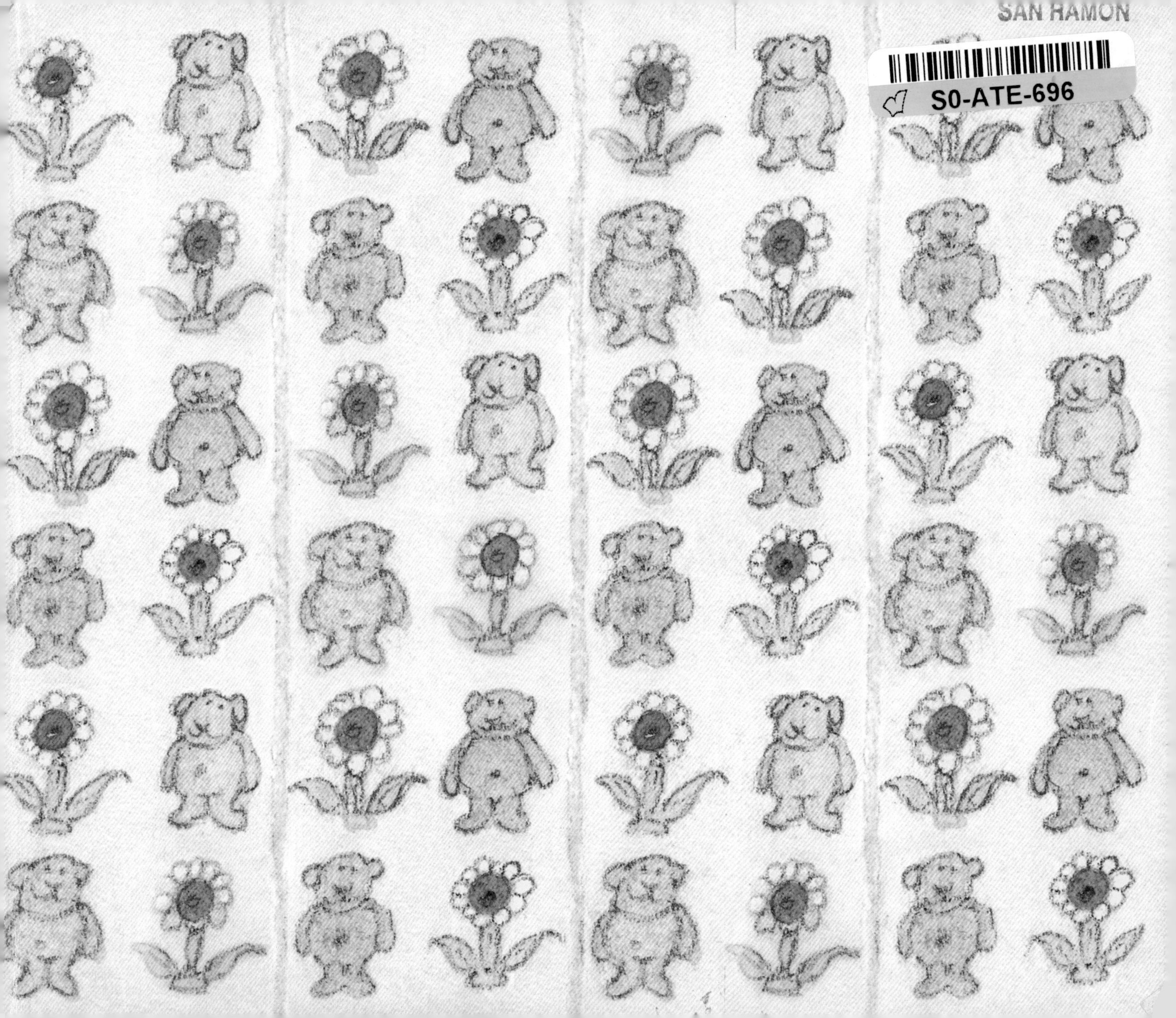

Bears
FOR RUTH & DAVE M.S.

story by Ruth Krauss
pictures by Maurice Sendak

Bears

Bears
Bears
Bears
WOW

Bears
Bears
GRRR

On the stairs

DUMB

Under chairs
HELLO?

Washing hairs

HA

Giving stares

YUM

Collecting fares
A-HA!
UH-OH
DOG STEALS BABY BEAR!

Stepping in

squares
?

Million

Million

squares
?

aires

Bears
Bears
Bears
WAH!

Bears
Bears

every

Bears
Bears

every

wheres

Hand lettering by Tom Starace
Library of Congress control number: 2004105682
Ruth Krauss's text for BEARS, *with pictures by Phyllis Rowand,*
was first published in 1948 by Harper & Brothers

Michael di Capua Books · HarperCollins Publishers

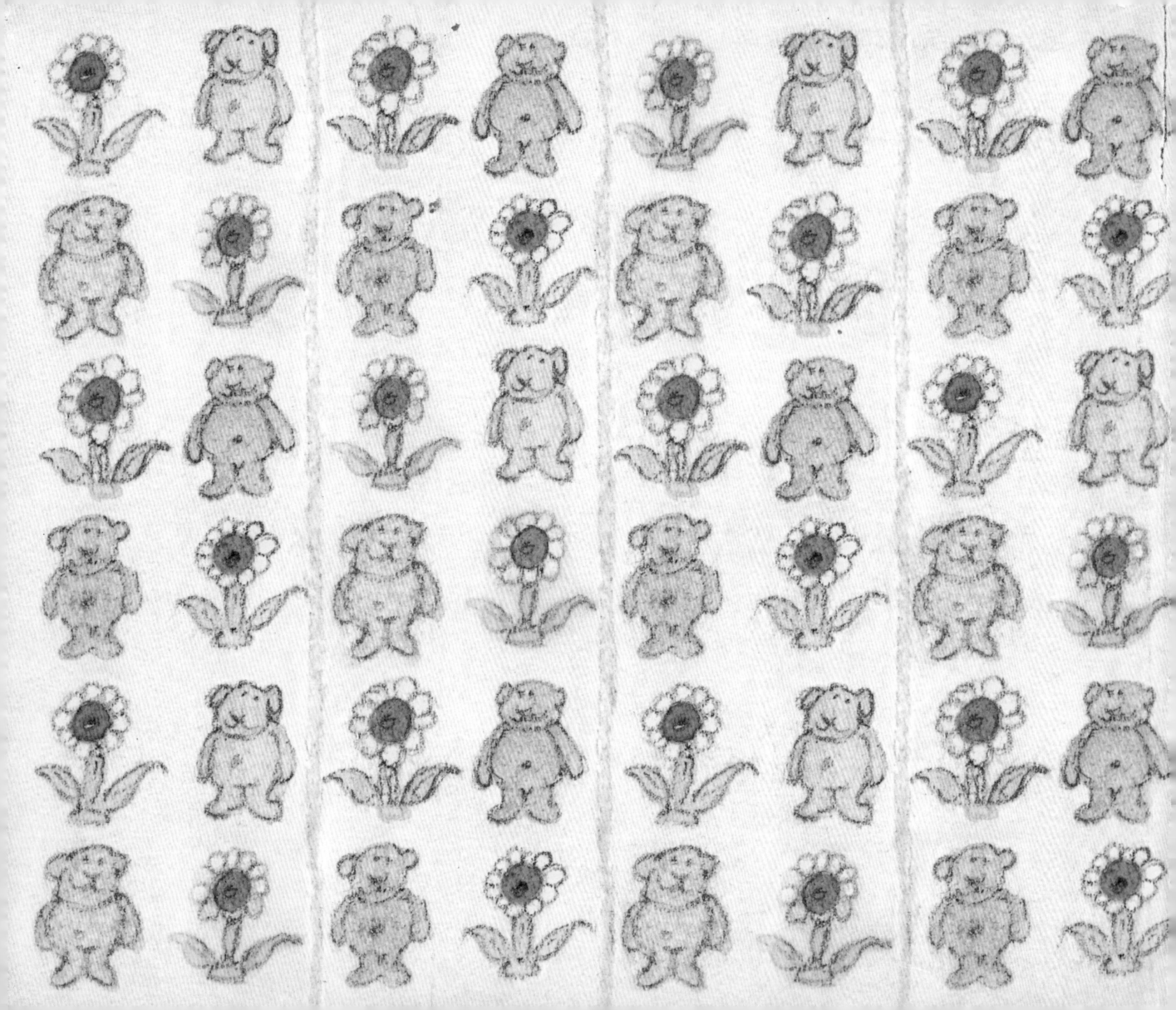